The Mystery of the Stolen Bike

An **ARTHUR** Chapter Book by **MARC BROWN**

ARTHUR
and the Mystery
of the Stolen Bike

Ⓛ Ⓑ

LITTLE, BROWN AND COMPANY

New York Boston

For my sister Kim,
and her family, Dave and Miles

Little, Brown and Company

Hachette Book Group
1290 Avenue of the Americas, New York, NY 10104
Visit our website at www.lb-kids.com

Little, Brown and Company is a division of Hachette Book Group, Inc.
The Little, Brown name and logo are trademarks of Hachette Book Group, Inc.

The publisher is not responsible for websites (or their content) that are not owned
by the publisher.

First Edition: March 2012
Originally published under the title *The Mystery of the Stolen Bike*

Arthur® is a registered trademark of Marc Brown.

Text by Stephen Krensky, based on the
teleplay by Kathy Waugh.

Library of Congress Catalog Card Number 98-65411

ISBN 978-0-316-13363-0

10 9 8 7 6

LSC-C

Printed in the United States of America

Chapter 1

• • • • • • • • • • •

The Frenskys were eating dinner in their apartment. At least Mr. and Mrs. Frensky and their older daughter, Catherine, were eating dinner. Their younger daughter, Francine, was not eating at all. She was just sitting in her chair with her arms folded.

"Francine's sulking," said Catherine.

"I am not," said Francine. "I don't even know what that means."

"It means you're a little, uh, out of sorts," said her father, Oliver. "A bit upset about not getting your way."

"Well, why shouldn't I be?" said Francine.

"I'm sorry, honey," said her mother, Laverne. "But we can't afford to get you a new bike right now. Maybe next year . . ."

Francine continued to sulk. "It's not fair. I'll just *die* without a bike."

Her father gasped. "No, say it's not true!" He dropped to one knee and grabbed Francine's hand. "You mustn't give up, honey. Live, I say, *live!*"

He would have continued, but Francine started to giggle. Pretty soon he was laughing himself.

"Oh, Dad," said Catherine, "do you really think a silly trick like that will work?"

Her father saluted her and stood up straight and tall. "Well, it worked on *you* when you were Francine's age." He stroked his chin. "But perhaps you're right. I don't know what came over me. Besides, I have an idea."

He got up from the table and held out his hand to Francine. "Come with me," he said.

They went down to the basement, where the Frenskys had a storage compartment. While her father unlocked it, Francine sat on the bottom step. She didn't see the point of coming down here. It was dark, there were cobwebs, and the air smelled a little funny.

"Aim that flashlight over this way," said her father.

Francine pointed the light toward the corner.

"That's better." Mr. Frensky rummaged around behind some boxes. "Aha! Here it is!"

He moved a box aside to reveal an old bicycle. Then he wheeled it over to her.

"Drumroll, please!"

Francine's face fell. This bike was not only old. It was also ugly. Bright purple

with chipped paint, rusted handlebars, and a glittery burnt-orange banana seat.

"What *is* it?" she asked.

"Your new bike," her father explained. "Well, actually it's an old new bike." He wiped off an enormous cobweb between the handlebars.

"Dad, bikes have changed a lot since the Stone Age."

Her father inspected it. "I don't know about that. They still have two wheels, a seat, and handlebars. And you don't see a banana seat like this every day. Definitely a collector's item."

"But I don't want a collector's item. I want a cross bike with twenty-one gears."

Her father laughed. "All those gears just get confusing. Three gears are plenty." He clicked through them as he spun the wheels. "All this needs is a little oil. It's in great shape. When I was your age, I rode it to school every day. I know you'll come to appreciate it as much as I did."

He patted the seat happily.

Francine just sighed. "If you say so," she said.

But she didn't have much hope.

Chapter 2

• • • • • • • • • • •

"It's not a bicycle," Arthur was saying. "Bicycles can't fly."

"Well, that's true," Buster admitted. They were talking about last night's episode of *The Bionic Bunny Show*. The bunny had a new vehicle for chasing villains and assorted bad guys.

"I never watch that show," said Muffy, locking up her bike. "There are much more educational and important things to watch."

"Like what?" Buster and Arthur said together.

"The Home Shopping Channel, of

course. If you don't pay attention to that, you can miss some really fabulous buying opportunities."

Buster rolled his eyes. "I'll take my chances," he said.

"Take your chances with what?" asked Francine as she rode up behind them and got off her bike.

Buster turned to her. "With skipping the Home Shopping —" He stopped talking and stared. "What's that you're riding?"

The others looked, too.

"Whoa!"

"Where are my sunglasses?"

"Ha, ha," said Francine. "This is my new bike."

Buster laughed. "New? In what century?"

"Too bad you couldn't get one like mine," said Muffy. She had the latest model: twenty-four gears, a graphite alloy frame, and radial brake pads.

"I could have had any bike I wanted," said Francine. "But I chose this one."

Muffy frowned. "But Francine . . . why?"

"Um, tradition. This bike was my dad's. It's like a family heirloom. He was able to do all kinds of tricks with it."

"I *guess* that makes it different," Muffy admitted. But she didn't look very convinced.

"The biggest trick," Buster whispered to Arthur, "will be if she can make it look any better."

Later that afternoon, the kids' teacher, Mr. Ratburn, was showing slides to the class.

"The wheel," he said, "is thought to have been invented approximately five thousand years ago in the Middle East."

"By the Sumerians or the Babylonians?" asked the Brain.

"I always get all those *-ians* mixed up," sighed Arthur.

"It is confusing," agreed Mr. Ratburn. "In this case I believe it was the Sumerians. Can anyone tell us what these ancient people might have done with their new wheel?"

Buster waved his arm wildly.

"Yes, Buster?"

"Built Francine's bicycle."

Everyone laughed—everyone but Francine and Muffy. Even after Mr. Ratburn ordered them to stop, a few kids continued to snicker.

"Stop picking on Francine," Muffy told Buster.

"Yeah!" said Francine.

"It's not her fault she has to ride an ugly, old bicycle," Muffy went on.

Francine blinked. "Oh?"

Muffy pressed her finger in Buster's

chest. "Just think how *you* would feel," she said.

Buster's face changed in mid-laugh. He looked embarrassed. So did everyone else. They got very quiet.

But none of them felt as embarrassed as Francine did, deep down inside where nobody could see.

Chapter 3

● ● ● ● ● ● ● ● ● ● ●

After school, Francine rushed outside while everyone else was still talking in the hall. She was mad and sad at the same time. This new bike was causing nothing but trouble. It was making everyone look at her differently. She wouldn't mind standing out for something special—like throwing a good fastball. But being teased and laughed at was no fun. It was no fun at all.

She went straight to the bike rack, half hoping that maybe this was all a bad dream.

But it wasn't a dream. And her bike

hadn't changed. It was still sitting there, in all its disgusting purple glory.

Why couldn't someone have come along and stolen it? she wondered. They had the whole day.

Well, even if no one had taken the bike, that didn't mean she had to keep looking at it. Glancing around, she noticed some bushes at the edge of the school yard. She wheeled the bike into them and rested it behind a garbage can.

For a moment, she thought the bike gave her a sad look.

"Don't worry," she whispered. "I'm not deserting you. Not yet, anyway. I just need some time to think. And it's better to not see you while I'm thinking."

Then she ran back to the front of the school.

Arthur, Muffy, and Buster were waiting for her. They all had their bikes and backpacks.

"Where were you?" Muffy asked. "You disappeared from class awfully fast."

Arthur poked Buster in the side. "Buster has something he wants to say to you, don't you, Buster?"

"Um, yes, I do," said Buster. He cleared his throat. "Francine, I'm sorry for what I said before. Insulting your bike, I mean."

"And we're sorry we laughed, too," said Arthur. "You know, my father has a beat-up frying pan from his early cooking days. It's all black, with a few dents and scratches. I once asked him why he didn't buy a shiny new one to use instead. He said there was something friendly about the old pan that just made food taste better. I'm sure your bike was like that for your dad."

Francine nodded. She felt a little better. "Thanks, Arthur," she said. "And you, too, Buster."

Muffy looked along the bike rack. "Where is your bike, anyway?" she asked.

"Oh, um, I'm not using it right at the moment. . . . I just feel like walking."

"We're going down to the Sugar Bowl," said Arthur. "Are you coming?"

Francine wasn't really in the mood. Even though she was glad her friends had apologized, she still felt out of place. Why did she have to be the one to stand out? She didn't want people to feel sorry for her—even if they *were* nice about it.

"Maybe I'll see you there later," she said.

Arthur shrugged. "Okay."

"Bye," said Muffy and Buster.

They all rode off, leaving Francine with her thoughts.

Chapter 4

• • • • • • • • • • •

That night Francine sat on the edge of her bed, bouncing a tennis ball on the floor.

Bounce. Bounce. Bounce. Bounce.

With every bounce, Francine wished for another bike. And not just any bike. A bike that would make Arthur and Buster wish they had one, too. A bike even Muffy would admire.

Her father popped in. "What's that noise? Oh, practicing your coordination, eh?"

"I guess."

"Practice is important. As your baseball coach, I can vouch for that. And speaking of coordination, how's the new bike? Seat the right height?"

"The bike is purple," Francine said dully. "Very purple."

Her father nodded. "That was my favorite color when I was your age. Purple is the color of royalty, you know. Dignified. Majestic."

"Really?" said Francine.

"Oh, yes. It was greatly valued in ancient times."

"You mean like back when they were inventing the wheel?"

"Exactly."

Francine sighed. "That figures," she said.

"So naturally it seemed like a great color to pick for a bike."

Mr. Frensky got a funny look on his face. Francine had seen it before. It was his boyhood-memories look. A story was bound to follow.

"Doesn't it ride great? Did you feel how it handles corners? I remember one time we were going to have a race through the neighborhood. I had never even come close to winning on my old bike. Then I got this one."

Francine stopped bouncing the ball. "What happened?" she asked.

"Well, we all lined up. And there was this one kid, a big bruiser, who was always bragging about how fast his bike was. You know the type. I wanted to beat him in the worst way."

Francine nodded.

"So the race starts, and I'm pedaling like crazy. And with the banana seat, I can really lean hard on the pedals. I'll never forget the look on some of the kids' faces as I passed them."

"So you won?"

Her father laughed. "Not exactly. The bruiser won—as usual. But at least I was

right in the middle. For me that was a big improvement."

"Oh."

Her father looked at her. "Don't look so disappointed, Francine. I was really happy just to do better."

"It wasn't that. I was wondering about . . ."

"Yes?"

"Well, you just said how exciting it was for you to get this new bike."

"Definitely. I thought my face was going to crack because I was grinning so widely."

"But don't you see? It was *new* for you back then. It's not new for me anymore. If I got a new bike, I could feel the same way you did."

Mr. Frensky sighed. "I wish I could get you a new one, honey. But we don't have the extra money right now. And my old bike has a long and proud history. I'm afraid that's going to have to satisfy you for now."

Francine started bouncing the ball again. She was a long way from feeling satisfied. A very long way. And from the way her father was talking, she could tell she wasn't going to get much closer anytime soon.

Chapter 5

· · · · · · · · · · ·

The next morning, Francine walked slowly to school. She had hoped that the start of a new day would make her feel better. But even though the sun was shining and the birds were singing, she felt just as bad as she had the day before.

As she turned the corner, up ahead she saw the bushes where she had hidden the bike. Her view, though, was partly blocked by a city garbage truck. The garbage collectors were out early, emptying the trash cans.

"Uh, oh!" she thought.

Just then, one of the men picked up Francine's bike and threw it into the truck.

Francine started to run.

"Hey! Hey!" she shouted, waving her arms. "Come back here! You've got my bike in there!"

But the collectors couldn't hear her over the roar of the truck's engine. They pulled away before she could get their attention.

Francine came to a stop. She was breathing hard. This was terrible! The bike was gone. What was she going to do now? She could only imagine what her father would say.

As she entered the school yard, Buster and Arthur zoomed up on their bikes. Arthur braked to a stop while Buster circled around them.

"Hey, Francine!" said Buster. "Want to do some wheelies before school starts?"

"I can't," said Francine. "I don't have my bike."

"Where is it?" asked Arthur.

"I don't know," she said. Even though she was partly glad to be rid of the bike, she didn't feel comfortable telling her friends what had happened.

"How can you not know?" asked Buster. He sometimes lost track of his stuff, too, but nothing as big as a bicycle.

Suddenly Francine had an idea. "My, um, bike was stolen," she explained.

"Stolen!" said Arthur. "Are you sure?"

"Of course she's sure," said Buster. "You don't make mistakes about something like that. Right, Francine?"

"Um, yes. I mean, I had it yesterday." She paused. "And now it's gone."

"Gone? What's gone?" said Sue Ellen, who was just arriving with Muffy.

"Someone stole Francine's bike," said Arthur.

"That's terrible," said Sue Ellen.

Muffy looked confused. "Why would anyone steal that — I mean, your bike?" she asked.

Francine shrugged. "It *was* pretty old . . ."

Muffy gasped. "Hey, *that* could be the reason! What if it was so old it was an antique?" She started waving her arms. "Help! Police!"

"What's going on?" asked the Brain, coming up behind them.

"Francine's bike was stolen," said Buster. "I'll bet it was a gang of international bike thieves. They're probably going to sell it on the black market."

"No, no," said Francine, who was beginning to think that saying the bike had been stolen wasn't such a good idea after all.

"Calm down," said Arthur. "Let's try not to panic."

"We should tell Mr. Haney," said the Brain.

"You're right," said Arthur. "Maybe we can still catch whoever stole it. They can't have gotten far."

"No! Wait!" said Francine. She didn't want to drag the school principal into this. But it was too late. All the other kids were running into the school.

All she could do was follow behind them.

Chapter 6

• • • • • • • • • • •

Mr. Haney looked hard at Francine from behind his desk.

"Let me get this straight," he said. "You were hurrying home on your bike yesterday to do your chores."

Francine nodded.

"And those chores would be?"

Francine thought for a moment. "Oh, you know, cleaning my room, helping to make dinner."

"Wow, I'm impressed," the Brain whispered to Buster. "I never hurry home to do my chores." They were standing behind Francine with Arthur and Muffy.

Mr. Haney scratched his chin. "And you were hurrying, you say?"

"That's right."

Francine could see herself riding along on her bike, whistling happily. All of a sudden a big truck came up behind her. It was kind of like a garbage truck, but with a big claw on the back.

The claw reached down and grabbed Francine's bike. She just managed to jump off before the claw lifted the bike up and dropped it into the truck.

Then the truck sped off, leaving Francine shaking her fist at it.

"I don't suppose you got the license plate number," said the Brain.

"Sorry," said Francine. "I thought I was lucky just to escape with my life."

Mr. Haney tried to look concerned. "I had no idea such trucks were roaming the streets. Giant claws, you say? I should report this to someone."

"We need to put out an APB!" said Buster.

"APB?" said Muffy.

"All Points Bulletin," Arthur explained.

Buster nodded. "The state police should blanket the highways. They should search every rest stop."

Listening to Buster, Francine found herself feeling more and more uncomfortable. "Um, Mr. Haney . . . I know the day hasn't really started yet, but can I go home? I don't feel very well.

"You do look a little pale," said Mr. Haney. "We'll have the nurse check you out. If she agrees, who should I call to come get you?"

Francine thought for a moment. "My mother, I think."

Mr. Haney nodded. "All right, Francine. Go wait in the nurse's office." He looked at the others. "The rest of you should get to class."

A little while later, Mrs. Frensky arrived to get Francine. As they were leaving, the other kids watched from the classroom window.

"Did you think there was something fishy about Francine's story?" asked Arthur.

"Fishy?" said Sue Ellen. "It sounded to me like Francine survived a terrible ordeal."

"Yeah," said Buster. "But take it from me, the story didn't add up. I mean, does Francine really expect us to believe she was hurrying home to do her chores? How dumb does she think we are?"

"I don't think Arthur meant that part," said Muffy. "I think he was referring to the bike-eating truck."

"All right," said Mr. Ratburn, "let's get back to work."

"Hmmm," said the Brain. "Such a truck

does seem a little unlikely. Is it possible she invented that part to keep us from finding out who really took her bike?"

"Why would she do that?" asked Muffy. "Shouldn't whoever took it be punished?"

"Unless . . . ," said Buster. "Unless the thief is somebody *we all know*."

The others opened their eyes wide. You're right," said Arthur. "We hadn't thought of that."

Chapter 7

• • • • • • • • • • •

That night the Frenskys were sitting in the living room, watching TV.

"Dad," said Francine, "I have something to tell you."

"Uh-huh," said her father. When he was watching TV, it was sometimes hard to get through to him.

"It's about my bike," Francine went on.

"Your bike," Mr. Frensky repeated.

Francine took a deep breath. "It's been stolen," she said. "There was this truck with a giant claw and I was knocked off and I'm lucky to be alive."

"Uh-huh," said her father.

"Goodness," said her mother, who was paying more attention. "What a close call. That sounds unbelievable."

"You're not kidding," said Catherine as she painted her fingernails.

Francine squirmed in her chair.

"Giant claws?" her sister continued. "Were you in some kind of super spy movie?"

"You don't know everything!" said Francine. "And you weren't there."

"That's enough, Catherine," said Mrs. Frensky, "Francine's had a tough day. She got sick at school . . ."

"Not very," said Catherine. "It's not like she threw up or anything."

"Even so, you're not helping. Concentrate on your nails. I think you missed a spot."

"Where?" asked Catherine, frantically inspecting each finger.

Francine let out a deep sigh. "So you're not mad, Dad?"

Her father blinked. "Mad? About what?"

"About my bike being stolen."

Mr. Frensky looked like he was about to say something, but then he caught a look from his wife.

"I can't say I'm happy, Francine," he said after a moment. "That bike held a lot of memories for me. But it must be hard for you, too, thinking about someone stealing your bike. But don't give up hope. Maybe it will find its way back to us somehow."

Catherine rolled her eyes. "Dad, it's a bike, not a dog. Anyway, I think some-one in this room knows more than she's saying."

Francine got up quickly. "I'm going to bed," she said. "I need extra rest if I'm going to get better."

She gave each of her parents a kiss good night, stuck out her tongue at her sister, and left the room.

As Francine was brushing her teeth, she looked in the mirror. She saw Catherine coming up the stairs behind her.

"Sticking your tongue out may make you feel better," said Catherine, "but it doesn't change anything. I want to hear more about what happened. Did you go right to the police?"

"I would have," Francine said back. "But . . . but I, ah, hit my head when I fell off my bike and got amnesia. By the time my memory came back, it was too late to catch anyone."

"That's from the movie we saw last week," said Catherine. "You'll have to do better than that if you want a new bike."

Francine didn't want to hear any more. She shut the bathroom door firmly.

"Go away!" she ordered.

She finished washing up and went straight to bed. For a long time she stared at the ceiling, imagining that at any moment a giant claw would crash through and grab her. But it never did, and finally she fell asleep.

Chapter 8

· · · · · · · · · · · ·

As Francine was walking to school the next morning, Buster and Muffy met her on their bikes.

"We've got news!" said Buster. "Big news!"

"About what?" Francine asked.

"About the crime of the century!" said Buster.

"What Buster is trying to say," said Muffy, "is that we think we know what happened to your bike."

Francine frowned. "But I already told you what happened. There was this truck, and—"

Muffy held up her hand. "Nice try, Francine, but you don't fool us."

"I don't?"

"Francine, we're your friends. We can tell when you're telling the truth."

"You can?"

Buster nodded. "Of course. That's how we know you made up that truck business. And we even know why."

Francine was beginning to feel a little dizzy. "You do?"

"It's because you're trying to protect someone," said Muffy.

Buster took out a drawing and showed it to Francine.

"The guys who swiped your bike, did one of them look like this?"

"Buster, that looks like Binky."

"We know," Buster said.

"It wasn't Binky," said Francine.

"But it has to be," said Buster. "Who else is big enough to steal a whole bike?"

"Never mind," said Francine. "Can't you just forget about it? It's none of your business, anyway."

Muffy looked hurt. "We're only trying to help," she said.

"Well, don't," Francine told her. "Just leave me alone."

She walked away, leaving Muffy and Buster behind her.

"What do you think?" asked Buster.

"I think she's being very brave," said Muffy. "But an injustice has been done. And we have to make it right."

A little while later, Muffy was standing in front of a bunch of kids. She was waving Buster's poster.

"I say Binky's behind it," she told the crowd. "And we have to make him confess."

"How?" asked the Brain.

"We could threaten him," said Muffy. "Any volunteers?"

Nobody answered. How could they threaten Binky? He was the biggest kid in the class.

"You're such a bunch of babies," Muffy went on. She didn't notice that Binky was walking up behind her.

"Um, Muffy!" said Arthur.

"Don't interrupt. One of my best and truest friends has been traumatized," she continued, sniffing a little. "This deed cannot go unpunished. And if it takes a Crosswire to fight this terrible wrong by herself, then so be it. It won't be the first time, and it won't be the—"

"Hey!" Binky called out.

Muffy turned.

Binky glared at her. "Are you telling everyone I stole Francine's bike?"

"What if I am? Feeling guilty about it?"

"No. Because I didn't take it."

"Then who did?" Muffy demanded. "Do you have a better idea?"

Binky shrugged and shook his head. "No, I just know it wasn't me."

"Stop it!"

Francine was shouting from the back of the crowd. "Stop picking on Binky. He didn't do anything."

Binky grunted. "Like I said."

"Then what happened to your bike?" asked Muffy.

"It . . . it got picked up with the trash by accident," Francine said quietly.

Muffy dropped the poster.

"Francine!" she cried. "Why didn't you tell us?"

Francine didn't know what to say.

"I'm sorry, Binky," said Muffy. "Can you ever forgive me?"

"And me, too," said Buster.

Binky shrugged. "Sure," he said. "I'm a tough guy, remember?"

Then he walked away.

Muffy sat down on the ground. "All of a sudden, I don't feel very good."

Francine nodded. "Join the club," she said.

Chapter 9

• • • • • • • • • • •

The sun was setting as Francine and her father started off for the dump. Francine had wanted to tell her father that the thieves had dropped her bike there to throw the police off their trail. However, when she had tried this story out on Catherine, her sister couldn't stop laughing.

"That's so ridiculous," Catherine had told her. "Even for you."

In the end Francine had called her father at work and told him the truth.

"Dad, it wasn't thieves," she had told him over the phone. "It was an accident."

"I see," her father had replied quietly.

"I guess if you were really being technical, you could say it was my fault."

"I'm glad to hear you admit it."

"You are?" Francine had been surprised. "You mean you knew already? But you didn't say anything?"

"Because I wanted you to say something first."

"Oh."

"And I'm proud that you did. Of course, I'd still like you to explain why you did it."

"Because everyone was making fun of me. But I didn't try to throw the bike away. I was just hiding it for a little while. And then when the garbage truck picked it up, I thought it might have solved my problem."

"And did it?"

Francine shook her head. "No. Things only got worse and worse."

"I can understand how you felt. But it's no excuse for lying about it."

"I know, Dad. I guess I didn't want to hurt your feelings. I knew how much the bike meant to you. I'm really sorry. What do we do now?"

"We go to the dump," Mr. Frensky had said on the phone.

And now here they were. Mr. Frensky asked the guard a question, and he pointed them toward the fresh trash.

"Now what?" asked Francine.

"We go hunting," said her father.

"You mean we have to—"

Her father nodded. "Consider it part of your punishment, young lady. At least the bike is big enough to stand out."

Francine started poking through the garbage with a stick. There were old pizza boxes and banana peels and broken toys to push aside.

The smell was awful. Francine tried holding her breath, but that didn't work very well. She settled for holding her nose and taking as few breaths as possible.

"I think I'm going to faint," she said.

"If you do," said her father, "who knows *what* you'll fall in."

"Good point," said Francine. Maybe fainting wasn't such a good idea.

"Aha!" said Mr. Frensky. He bent down and pushed aside some crumpled papers and cups. "Look, here it is!"

He pulled the bike up and out.

One good thing about an old bike, thought Francine, is that it can sit in the dump overnight and not look any worse.

"Did you really ride that thing to school every day?" she asked.

Her father smiled. "Uphill both ways."

Francine looked at the bike with new respect. "Wow. Hey, maybe we could fix it up."

Her father shrugged. He took out a rag and began wiping the bike off.

"How about it, Dad? All it really needs is some new paint."

Mr. Frensky looked at Francine. "Well . . ." He grinned broadly. "What are we waiting for?"

Chapter 10

• • • • • • • • • • • •

Outside the Frenskys' apartment, the whole family was standing ready.

"Why do *I* have to be here?" Catherine asked.

"You're part of the family," said her mother. "And this is a family moment."

"I was afraid you'd say that," Catherine muttered.

In front of them, a white bedsheet had been draped over the old bike, which Francine and her father had been working on for a week.

"This better be good," said Catherine.

"Ladies and . . . ladies," said Mr. Fren-sky, looking around. "We'd like to present Francine's new and improved, completely restored . . ."

He pulled off the sheet.

". . . bicycle!"

Francine and her mother clapped.

The new bike was brightly painted. It was still purple, but now it gleamed like a star. And the banana seat had been rubbed and polished, restoring the luster to the old vinyl.

"Beautiful!" said Mrs. Frensky. "Oliver, you and Francine did a wonderful job."

Francine beamed.

"Thank you, thank you," said her father. "I have to confess that the finishing touch, the racing stripes on the fenders, were Francine's idea."

"Nobody else has anything like them," said Francine. "Not even Muffy."

"I like the color," Catherine admitted.

"In fact," she added, holding out her hand, "it might look good on my nails."

"Well, Francine," said her father, "praise doesn't come any higher than that." He paused. "And now the moment of truth— the test drive. Francine, will you do the honors?"

He bowed and stepped aside. But Francine held out her helmet.

"You first, Dad."

"Are you sure? I wouldn't want to deprive you of your big moment."

Francine smiled. "I'm sure."

Mr. Frensky took Francine's helmet and strapped it on.

"Be careful, honey!" said Mrs. Frensky.

He waved her worries aside. "Don't worry, dear. Riding a bicycle is like, well, riding a bicycle. You never forget how."

"Maybe so," said Catherine, "but don't let anyone see you, *please*."

"I'll do my best. Just a little spin around

the block. I want to make sure it's absolutely safe."

He mounted the bike and wobbled down the sidewalk. As he rounded the corner, he stopped to make sure he was out of sight. Then he pushed off fast and whizzed down the street, his face lit up with glee.

"Do you think he'll be okay?" asked Catherine as her father disappeared from sight.

"Of course," said Francine. If this whole experience had taught her anything, it was that she could always count on her dad.